Dedicated with love
to my three beautiful daughters,
Stacey, Samantha and Shannon,
and to all little boys and girls everywhere
and their Mommies and Daddies,
who share in the excitement
of their children's
first day at
school.

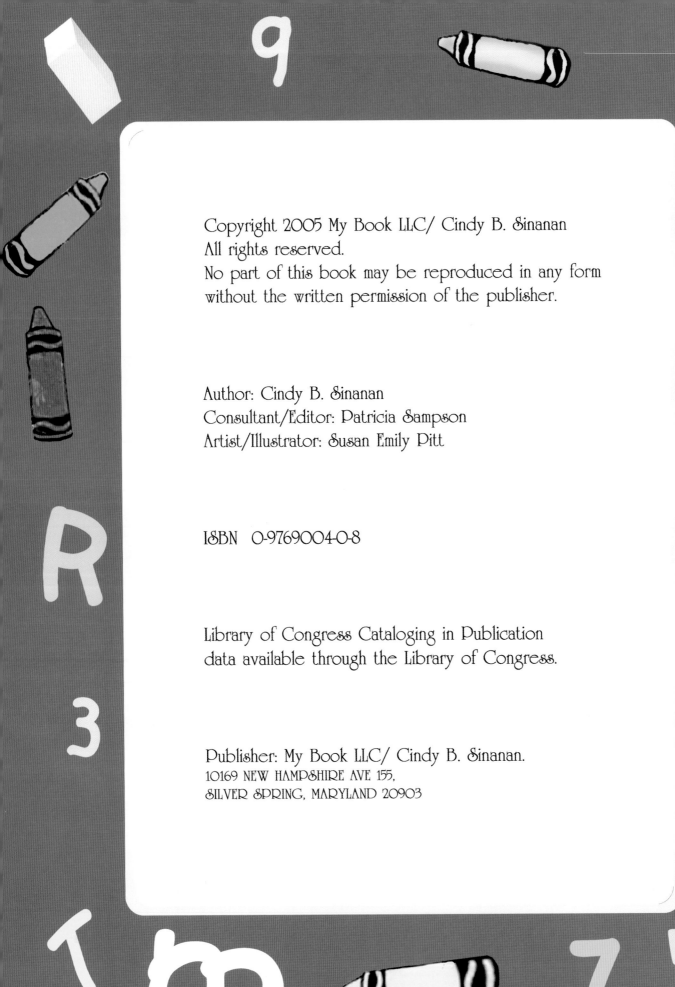

Author: Cindy B. Sinanan
Consultant/Editor: Patricia Sampson
Artist/Illustrator: Susan Emily Pitt

ISBN   0-9769004-0-8

Library of Congress Cataloging in Publication
data available through the Library of Congress.

Publisher: My Book LLC/ Cindy B. Sinanan.
10169 NEW HAMPSHIRE AVE 155,
SILVER SPRING, MARYLAND 20903

MY BOOK LLC.
Silver Spring, Maryland 20903

Stacey wakes early
and greets the day.
"This is my first day
of school.

Hooray!

All summer long
I could
hardly wait~
I know that school
will be so
great!"

Stacey clasps
her hands
tightly
and says
a little prayer.
"Please...
take away
my butterflies,
before
I get there!"

Stacey brushes
her teeth
while Mommy
hugs her
tight.
"Ready for your
first day,
Honey?"
" Yep Mommy.
I'm alright."

9

Mommy brushes
her hair
until
it shines.
It looks pretty
and feels so fine.
Stacey feels proud
of her dress
all in blues,
her beautiful bow
and shiny
new shoes.

A healthy
breakfast before
going her way,
her backpack
filled for
an exciting day!
With fat pencils,
crayons,
erasers too,
shiny paper
and sparkly glue.

Stacey
and Mommy
set out to walk.
Along the way
they have
time to talk.
"Anything you
don't understand,
don't be afraid
to raise
your hand."

"Bye, Mommy,
I love you!"
Stacey joins
the new kids
and her
teacher, too.
The children
are excited
to begin the day,
and hear what
the teacher
has to say!

"Boys and Girls
you all are here
to begin school
~ an exciting year!
Find a chair
and sit down,
please,
it's time
to become
busy bees."

19

"In Grade One
you'll have
real fun
and learn all
you need
~to write
and to count ~
and best of all.
.. READ!"

The children
did the best
they could,
as their teacher
knew they would.
Stacey showed
her page
to Grace.
"Mr Mark
gave me
...a smiley face!"

22

The day
was over
far too fast!
Stacey wanted
the fun to last.
Numbers, letters,
colors
and shapes
~school is such a
WONDERFUL
place!

24

"Mommy,
I loved today.
I listened
to what
my teacher
had to say.
We sounded
out letters the
grown-up way...
and then we all
went out to play."

"Mommy,
when I'm bigger,
could I
write a book?
It would be
so exciting
to give other
kids a look,
at what goes on
inside Grade One,
so they will know
it's so much fun!"

28

29

The first day is over.
All snug in her bed,
visions of
schoolwork
dance in her head!
Stacey dreams
of tomorrow,
while cuddling Ted,
excited and happy
for school days
ahead!

31

School is fun!